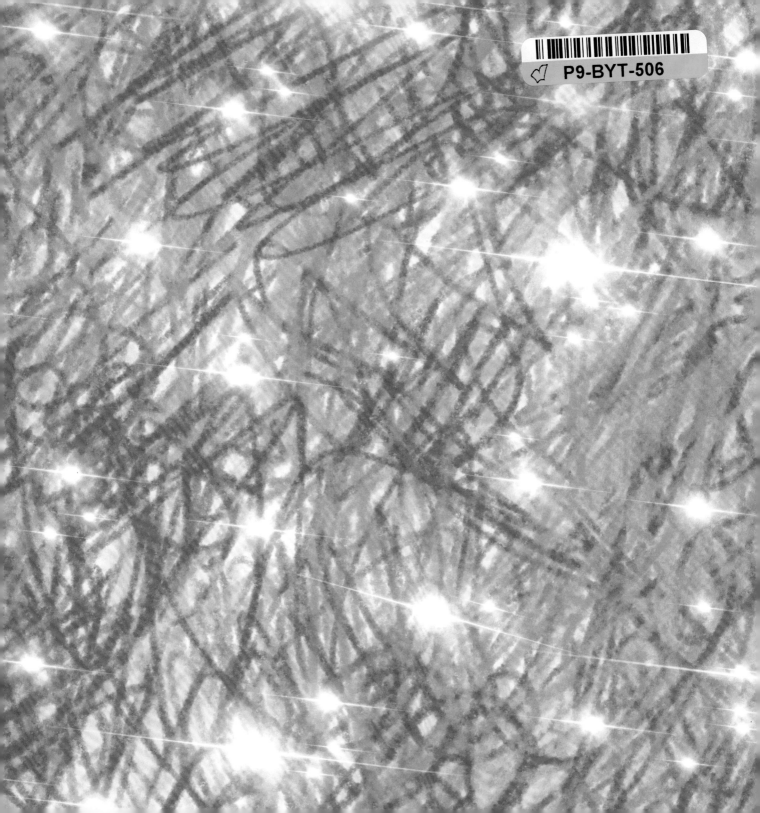

This book belongs to:

Evie L.H.

To my daughter Anna.

Who LOVES to scribble with her unicorn.

NEVER LET A UNICORN SCRIBBLE!

Written & Illustrated by
Diane Alber

I recently got a pet unicorn. I know it's hard to believe, but it's true. And everyone keeps telling me, **NEVER LET A UNICORN SCRIBBLE!**

Why would anyone say such a thing?
I mean, unicorns can run on rainbows,
so why can't they scribble?

I thought if I gave her just ONE crayon,

what could go wrong?

Well...I'll tell ya...

SHE ATE IT!

Now my favorite bright pink crayon was
traveling to the belly of my unicorn. This is probably why
people are saying unicorns should NEVER scribble.
Because they EAT crayons!

Then it occurred to me:

"Maybe unicorns don't know how to use crayons?"

So I gathered all my crayons and started to scribble.

I made a blue scribble, a pink scribble, a yellow scribble,

and even a **CRAZY** scribble!

Now that she could see how crayons worked,
I thought I would give her another chance to scribble.

I took out a **teal** crayon and placed it right in front of her...

AND SHE ATE HALF OF IT!

"Listen to me Unicorn,

WE DO NOT EAT CRAYONS!

We draw with them!"

But then I realized a unicorn couldn't hold a crayon like I could. Maybe that was why she was eating them!

I had an idea...

Maybe if I tied a few crayons to her horn
that would help her scribble!

Within seconds, glitter scribbles started

shooting out like water
from a firehose!

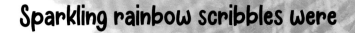

Sparkling rainbow scribbles were

EVERYWHERE!

They were on the floor, on the ceiling, on the walls! They were even on my lamp!
I've been begging my mom to redecorate my room for awhile now, but I don't think this is what she had in mind.

Then I heard a noise down the hall...This was it!
I was going to be in so much trouble!
I popped out of my room and blocked the door.
Before my mom could say anything, I started
to explain the mess she was about to see...

"Well, it all started when I heard to never let a unicorn scribble.

But I had to find out why. So I gave my unicorn a crayon, and then she ate it! Then I tried to TEACH her to scribble, but then she ATE ANOTHER CRAYON!

So I tied the crayons to her horn, and boy was that horn magical! The scribbles started shooting out like a water fountain and they were SO sparkly...

but it made such a mess...and...I'm sorry."

My mom peeked around the corner and smiled, "You didn't make a mess! You made a glowing masterpiece!"

When I turned around, all the scribbles were right on my easel. Not on the ceiling, not on the walls, not on my lamp. They were all on one big piece of paper, and it was the most amazing art ever!

All this time people wanted to stop unicorns from scribbling. It could be because they eat crayons. Or because it's so messy. But if my unicorn had never scribbled, she would have never learned how to make this masterpiece! So the next time you hear, a unicorn shouldn't scribble, just remember...

All great art starts with a scribble...
and even unicorns have to start somewhere!

The End.